ENDURANCE

THE SURVIVOR

LANCY CHOPRA

ॐ भूर्भुवःस्वःतत्सवितुर्वरेण्यं

भर्गो देवस्य धीमहि धियो यो नः प्रचोदयात् ॥

Contents

Foreword

When there is no fear of losing, then, discover to obtain...

-thehomelycurls

Preface

Ever remember the past while sitting in the examination hall? Have you ever noticed that new ideas are either manifest in the bathroom or during exam time? Well! While sitting in the examination hall, I have sketched my plans countless times. Yet, those plans got changed several eras of it before exiting the examination hall.

Hi! I'm Lancy Chopra. Most of you know me by my channel name –thehomelycurls. And some of you call me Lance.

One day while editing another draft, I clicked out an idea for a new short story. This story is so tremendous that I fancied it worth sharing with you before I publish my other books. The endurance word is self-vestige, the power of patience. This piece of fiction is not claiming any religion, gender or authenticity. This work is only impersonating how a person could fight under its circumstances.

Model credit goes to my little wonder world Priyanshika Chopra. She inspires me every time when ever I feel diversion.

Join me and live 'You in my words.'

All the pictures used in this book are entitled to personal and copyright @ Lancy Chopra.

MODEL : PRIYANSHIKA CHOPRA.

CHAPTER ONE

Examination hall

I diligently memorised the crooked script inked in the book, but within a few milliseconds, these phrases came out of my mind, annoyed. The thundering outside made it hard for me to concentrate on the tilted-headed letters. I pretty much like to see these petite shower drops falling on the glass windows but regret that today cannot live this felicitous moment. I cannot capture the picture of outward movements by taking a glance at the camera of my eyes.

She is sitting in front of us, monitoring us. Scary eyes, extraordinarily spooky. All the time, filled with rage, used to find flaws in all of us and ready to punish. I have been afraid of them ever since we first met. The first day of my school became the lesson of my crowning year. Does not know what colour this meeting will show today.

As I stepped into the examination hall, noticing Miss Bhandari, I forgot all about the preparation for my presentation. It was fundamental; at first, she was terrified by her personality. Also- a half-hour earlier, Cathy further frightened me with the story of what happened four days earlier while boarding the bus.

Discussions happen continual about Miss Bhandari, but from what I heard today, I can still feel the impact as a shiver in my veins.

Miss Bhandari is called in this school by the name of Miss Fear. Apparently, this eight-year-old child urinated out of the corridor because of this dread, which resulted in embarrassment. He did not come to school for the last four days after the nagging by some students.

Besides, we determined that Miss Fear terror is no scarcer among the school staff. Her scolding sometimes also caused fever for the other teachers.

In this claptrap environment on campus, I miss my old school enormously; how we used to have fun without fear, how lovingly and freely used to talk to our teachers. Even if kids occur mistakes, the teacher takes care of them as a mother. And if that mother got angry, the principal would convince her like a grandmother.

But one night, everything switched abruptly. Luck changes in a moment, and so does the person; we learn the value of these words in the iniquity of the same night. That night covered the fate of our family with its deep black sheet.

It was the night of 31st December, and the world was busy celebrating the New Year. The snow on the white sheet was the glory of our courtyard, and the black crown turban increased the pride in the sky's head. That day's beauty was not limited to this. During the New Year celebration, firecrackers were shining along stars together the crown of the sky. That scene was adorable. We were going to step into the flight of countrymen. We; Clueless dreamers. Without knowing it, someone else is sowing the foundation of their cruel intentions on our premises. Over; two minutes-- and the rest were in the show of giant firecrackers-- like a mouth-opened dragon into the sky.

It was only two minutes, which was the life of the residents there. At noon, the sky illuminated, filled with colour, and the white sheet filled with blood. The next daylight left us nowhere, and the darkness of fear settled in our hearts. A few unfortunate people like me survived to tell this story.

Everyone's turn is happening one by one. Soon it will be my deed to read the presentation. I'm scared virtually.

There is no point in looking into whether I will do this or not. Have to do it, however; I made myself ready.

Time teaches you everything- this proverb my father always spoke to me. But my mother used to say -learn from time. No one will come to instruct.

The identical thing happened that day. When my eyes opened in the morning, I was lying on a naked ice hone. Perhaps that soft padded snow probably melted and hardened because of me lying there overnight. I endeavour to get up, but it was arduous to lift my body. I tried to call a shout for help, but my scream didn't reach my ears, so how would anyone else reach me? It also swelled the tongue benumbed, causing complexity in breathing.

The time had taught-- a night before, a naughty girl child used to play, tease everyone, and she could not come under control by anyone. Today, she lay forlorn and incapable of laying down on the wet, cold earth.

I tried to look around, turning my eyes. Everywhere the vermilion of snow and bricks of stone were crushed. My hopes were broken. When I tried to look at the other side, I spotted someone. Someone looked like me, also lying on the ground. It was like Broken-straw-support. But the difficulties did not end. I stuck there, my shivering body and tongue-tied voice; how to help myself?

The proverb spoken by the father had come true, but it turned out to be ineffective. Now the time has come- to understand and learn the mother's statement.

The weather slowly started changing. Chilly winds with thunderstorms. Whether it rains or snow acquiesces, both of them will go cold in the winter. I would have to get up anyway - decided in mind and started dragging myself to the side where I regarded that person. With only a few distances and centuries of hard work, one can discern the same on which my condition was once.

Hardly could I have covered some distance, but nature's havoc was still there. The sky was striving to decorate the soft snow cotton on the earth with its fingers. If I had not been in that helpless condition, of-course, I would have been playing with the wings of that snow. But for the first time, I had a fright of being hit by ice. The fire inside me gave me the strength to fight against the chilly winds. The snow kept falling on me, and I, falling, took myself to that person.

For the first time, my own body was a burden to me, but I took to the person with hard work and hope.

When I viewed the person up close, my eyes were set free from questions. Before that, I would have been disappointed or let the icy breeze settle the tears on my cheeks; I had learned a lesson from the time. If my mother knew this, she would be proud of me.

I did not take the time to cut the innocence in my eyes, and then the slag of animalism trickled out through my eyes. That person had lost his strength even before I reached there. Either he gave up, or his God called him.

Winter was growing, and in the battle to save me, my innocence was dying. I underwent that step, which rarely if this society -- which explains humanity-- accepts. To date, it was known and understood that on the dead body -shroud, sheet, or whatever name given-the cloth offered on its new and final journey. But I took off the warm clothes from the dead body of that person and wore them myself.

Proud of such humanity, which became salutary to others even after their death.

I do not know how long the snow kept falling, and I kept looking at that angelic psyche to save myself.

Finally, God blessed me as the golden sun rose from the sky and kissed my swollen-closed eye. I had learned from a time when there were piles of dead bodies, but I was alive. Life has chosen me.

I had to live to thank the sacrifice of the person with whom I took clothes. I have to get out of there now. There is another village down the hill, and there I have to go and ask someone for help; keeping this hope, I started moving my steps.

While leaving, I stopped for two moments to thank that person, to say a final goodbye to him. Taking a pledge not to return to that place, I started my new journey from there.

CHAPTER TWO

The Fighting Spirit

You do not panic eying me; I am also a child like you.

Yes, I was a child, though my childhood had ended up a few miles behind. The blood on my face and the innocence on that child's face; was the difference between him and me. I moved from my hamlet, - the name of which village is probably no longer on the map of this world; at that time, I was a junior nine-year-old doll of my parents, who had become an orphan of nine years while travelling for a few hours. On my face- there was an opened mirror of malaise and cruelty, considering that the fear of that child was natural.

I should wash my face before asking for help. I smell terrible blood. But there was no water anywhere. Perhaps that child may have come far away from his village. I could not even perceive any house in that place. Before I could ask him anything, he dashed away from considering my condition.

While escaping, I came from my village to here, and he sailed away after glancing at me - maybe this was the decision of nature for me.

I was thirsty and famished; beating with pain, struggling to live; but I am still alive today. That's the truth.

I am alive because I did not stop that day. When I swore not to look back, I followed that protocol. Sometimes walking in the cold, sometimes falling, sometimes crawling, without stopping, I continued to rip through the jungles of the hills. Along with the burden of my body, I was carrying the load of many fears inside me.

Yes, I had a phobia - to go from freezing to burning with hunger and thirst, to spread the poison of my wounds - and many more. I needed strength to overcome all these weaknesses. But since yesterday, I have got nothing to eat yet. Mother not found, nor the courtyard in which she used to feed me with love.

I have to iterate here in the crematorium of this lush green field. This rate also started growing in my curiosity; whacked in the way, and is there any destination; I do not know it.

But it was moreover necessary to rest, so I sat there. While waiting, that child might bring someone to help me. Maybe he told someone about me? Hope teaches man the way to live.

From night to morning, I learned many rules of life. Now I was not the girl who was afraid of the dark.

This queen daughter of the father used to shout 'Papa, Papa' whenever the light of the room went out, and the father also quickly came to lit the flame on his magic wand and illuminated the room again.

But on that night, I did not call him. On that night in the jungle, I kept going in a silent arc. Noiselessly.

It is only the right to remain silent in the forest. You do not want animals to be aware of your arrival.

But I also witnessed the magic wand that night, someone holding it in their hands. He lit a fire by burning some wood on the ground. At some distance, the others were standing near the clothing camp with a flambeau. I hid behind that thick tree trunk for a while. That scene did not look like a tourist camping.

I should have left from there, but the aroma of the cooked food stopped me there for a while.

I wanted to have food, thought of going to them, and went ahead a few steps. But I took a step back when I saw a gun in a person's hand. Yes, it was a gun; I have seen it at the cinema many times. My father has shown many patriotic films.

But he was not a soldier. I could sense from his words.

They were the same people who destroyed my house and ended the fortune of many people like me. But I will not give my future to these predators. But in this condition and at this age, I can do nothing wrong with them. Keeping this in mind, I returned.

Leaving from there was not my cowardice. It was prudent.

I didn't get food from there, but I had heard of some secret that gave me a chance to live. I perceived a direction where I would go after coming out of here alive.

Before I can help the country, at the moment, I need help. I don't know when my hope will be over and when that child will bring an angel to help me.

Ought to step. This dryness in the throat will not be more tolerable. Now it is not a skilful act to wait too much. It is more beneficial to go ahead.

If I give up because of tiredness, the soul will end up with the body. If I endure, moving might find a well or a spring.

Nature will not be going to come to me; I have to pace. So much was going on in my core.

Yes. I dared. It was necessary. By taking small steps, the force I have folded some distance.

Where was I going? -Had no idea; there was no picture or name as addressed as my destination.

I did not discover the village I wanted to go to; I had gone with my daddy a long time ago, whose path I did not attain.

I got lost in a deserted way. Whether I was moving forward or rounding in the same way, that was not even becoming acquainted. Have to proceed- I was yelling into my mind; doesn't know which direction because zero would go to get by stopping.

So keep moving, keep actuating again after getting weak. But I was disappointed because I did not get water.

It started getting evening; the cold was accumulating. And the thundercloud wept over my condition.

When HE gives, HE gives it thatch; the same thing happens. HE rained, HE rained heavily, as HE could not tolerate my search for water.

This time, nature came to me.

After drinking the same rainwater, I quenched my thirst. And after cleaning myself with the same water, I climbed the tree.

During the night, not only the effulgence firefly illuminates the sky but also the wild animals go out for hunting -Mother always used to recite such stories.

Time never stops for anyone; we get exasperated. But my spirits were not enervated; till.

I was feeling sleepy. Also, there was a pile of blood loss, but I didn't want to sleep.

I was afraid that if I slumber, and didn't wake up again ever; then?

"Anyhow night shall pass, and then in the morning, I will put on my quest for my destination." I pondered on that time.

My story could have taken a few more turns if it had not happened.

Avoiding the animals of the land, the tree on which I was resting, there was someone else too. Black tickling crawled on the same branch. Perhaps angry because I entered its house without knocking.

It gazed at me and turned speedily towards me. That at the dread, my hand slipped, and I fell. The sound of my fall awakens many more animals. The sound of an owl, the barking of dogs, and umpteen different voices began to appear.

Once again, the fear had lifted the courage in me, and I moved; though the speed was sore dead, it was terribly arduous.

I thanked the snake in my mind- due to its fear, I waft so far. After all, there was a village in front of my eyes. In the quiet corridors, the lightning of a house that illuminated my hope was flickering in my eyes.

When a butterfly plays on a flower in the garden, it is reassuring to watch it; at that moment was bringing, I undergo the same feeling.

When Diwali is to come, so the list of how many dishes we prepare in our mind? My long journey was home to Diwali. In pursuance of the hope, my keen appetites start becoming a bit awake again. Just a few more steps, just a few more steps; the stomach begins to sing.

I learned courage and positivity from my time. Without thinking about whether anyone will help me- my emotions were playing Holi indeed in an account of prior ecstasy to get help.

CHAPTER THREE

New Phase

Who are you? Which religion are you? He asked this question first.

I knocked on the door of that house with great hope. Where I had so much patience, it was rigorous to wait for a few moments.

Someone came out and hooked me to the chest; I knew it was hypothetical.

My mum used to smile as soon as she opened the door whenever I returned home. She came to me, used to take all my cries- but now love has gone by my life. But trust me, I have not given up hope of sympathy. I believed that whoever opened the door would pity me.

My father also shepherded the path of goodness and humanity. In a one-time stormy rain, a sick cat he brought into the house. We gave her warm milk and supported her to stay indoors overnight.

Well, I am a human being.

A middle-aged man opened the door. I smiled and said hello to him. But perchance, my wounds introduced me more than the truth of my eyes.

What happened to you? How did it happen? Who did it? He had nothing to do with words like these. It was vital for him to know what religion I am.

Mother used to say, never speak a lie, mislead no one. But this education, taught by my mom in this situation, may not work.

I did not know what house that stands for or what religion they believe-in.

I do not eschew any religion, but the situation did not set it upright for me to name any God at that time.

Fearing, I said, I do not know about Dharam. But yes, I know I am an Indian. I have often heard in my house 'Jana Gana Mana'.

Looking at him, he couldn't seem to agree with me. As much as I was afraid of my condition, he was much afraid of an immature girl. Without doing help, he asked me to leave. And speaking of this, he closed the door.

Presumably, he was right, but I was not wrong.

Despondent and with no choice, I lay down on the bench near that house. I wanted to go, but my emotions failed with hope and fatigue.

Again, with the hope, tomorrow morning, I will knock down the door of another house in this village. Perhaps some kind-hearted people will extend a helping hand.

The night had not yet passed, and humanity was still in that gratifying shape in him.

After a few moments, the same door opened again, and the same fellow holding something in his hands was coming toward me.

Because of my weakness, even my eyes became blurred, and because of this, I could not fathom the food plate.

Seeing him approaching, I stood up from the bench with exquisite respect. Before endowing the filled food plate into my hand, he said, dinner is over. There is some leftover rice from the breakfast. Eat if you want to eat. But with rice, I have only these salted onions to offer.

I had no words to thank him, so I tried to say 'thank you with a smile on my wounded face.

I stayed, took food in my hands, till he went back home.

Whenever I forgot to wash my hands before eating food, my mother always interrupt.- "You should thank before eating food; first the person who gave you food to eat and then the God who introduced you to those who have given you to eat."

The unique game is of nature; my everything, every relationship, home, village, and the full world of mine is over, but I still have to thank God for this meal.

Who once used to show tantrums about taste, today I am eating dull rice tastefully.

The lights of that house keep burning all night long, and the person sitting at that window kept watching me the whole time.

A priori, he was guilty that he did not let me enter his house in this inclement weather. But it is also admissible; because this is not appropriate to trust an unknown and let them get on the premises by keeping faith at midnight. Yet he helped me; that was enough for me. The house stayed illuminated throughout the night, and I fixed my eyes on the window.

The following day had begun, and the village inaugurated a tweet with the noise of children. The sounds of utensils started coming from the houses, the same as they used to be in my village.

Mother, why do you bang the kitchen every morning? I have often asked these questions my mother, and the answer comes, I cannot beat you, that's why I am 'lamming the platters. Haha!! I only have memories now to express my impressionistic wealth.

Before anyone from the village would scrutinize me, the same person came in front of me who gave me food to helpless me last night. As soon as he arrived, he started a series of questions. Even though this time, the questions were the same, the style of asking was different.

"Have you come from the same village where the attacks took place yesterday?"

"Yes."

"Come with me to my house." And I followed. I went on thinking; how the man who had left me outside in a cold winter last night, is letting me enter his house in the morning?

But I don't know why I followed him without asking any questions. That should not have been but believing in him. Because he fed me last night may be the only reason for my faith in him.

It was an intimate house where entities were scattered. Witnessing the condition of the room, I understood that no one other than Uncle lived there. There was a table in front of which steam was coming out of the kettle lying on it.

"Sit down and have a cup of tea."

"Yes, sir."

The tea tasted great, merely like my father used to do to convince my mother; whenever she gets angry.

At last, he asked, "what happened?" The answer to this question was more consequential, so after drinking tea from comfort, I told the entire story beginning on the evening of 31st December.

We children were playing with snow, waiting for the night. Everyone knew that the firecrackers show would happen. Then we children observed an aged uncle. He had a quantity of luggage in his hand.

To help someone is the virtue of righteousness - this is what parents have taught.

Considering the condition of that uncle, he was looking exhausted and could not bear the weight of the goods he was holding in his hands. We went to him and assured him we would deliver his goods wherever he would like. After listening to us, he started blessing us.

Delivering New Year gifts home to home. It was easy for us. Our children took responsibility by holding each gift to reach their destination, and after the completion of work, we returned to the same playground.

On a gift, there was written my house address which I had on my hand.

I returned with a gift to my mother. My mother would also be busy at work, which is why she did not ask me anything, where a gift has come from and who gave it; if she had asked it, it would have been better.

As we kids had decided, I had to go back to the playground. When we all punters met; we told each other about the gifts, which had reached almost every one of our houses.

Somebody got sweets, some of them got toys, and don't know what else. But what did we all know? The stuff we are considerably amusing at getting has brought the gift of death.

All of us kids got busy playing. Hours passed, and it was time to return home. When I arrived home, I noticed the gift was lying with the rest of the endowments.

I wanted to open it, but my Mother interrupted and said to keep patience. We should open it after midnight. Let's devour the meal; then it will be time to burn the crackers.

None of us wanted to miss that show. After all, such a show had never happened in our village before, nor did anyone hear about it. At 11:45 PM, we were all on the roof. From then on, diminutive sky-shots started burning. The sky was decorated for a few moments with a procession of twinkling stars.

We were all enjoying that atmosphere. Then a voice came from under my courtyard, "Leela, come with us. You too let some big-one bing." It would be fun. I got out of the house in excitement with permission from my parents.

It left a time of two minutes for the firecrackers. I was walking on the earth and gazing at the azure. I must have reached some distance from the house only when the stars started glowing in the sky and with that, the gigantic explosion started.

It was all because of those rumble offerings. My friend, standing at a distance of about two hundred meters, was calling me with the same gift in his hand when suddenly all those houses started exploding. These eyes of mine have seen every house crumbling. My misfortune was that I was left alone, my house got slaughtered, my parents were killed, and my village had destroyed. If there was anything left, it was devastation and me.

CHAPTER FOUR

Leela Krishan

You appear excellent, but you look like a boy, the person who told me that is no longer unknown to me. He asked me after hearing about my journey that day. Where will you go now? I did not have an answer to this. So I took my breath and stayed quiet.

He asked again after a few moments. Would you like to be with your parents? Would you like to go to school, want to read, write, and have fun with friends? The question was inevitably emotional and beyond my comprehension. But I did not want to fabricate any argument on their incomplete talk, so I said to them, Sir, what do you want to say?

"Karam, you can call me Karam Uncle. You said, you do not know your religion, but you are Indian; that's when you knock my heart. I also do not believe in any religion. Dharam has divided humans, which is not admissible. The moment you clattered on the house, I was watching the news, where it was persisting in form, that children were also included in the terrorist rate. At the same time, I put you in the cold outside overnight. But keeping an eye on you, I became convinced that you are not a terrorist but a survivor. One of my relatives is in the army. His son lasted in the army and had proudly martyred for his country. My relatives are childless now if you want, you can assign them to your parents."

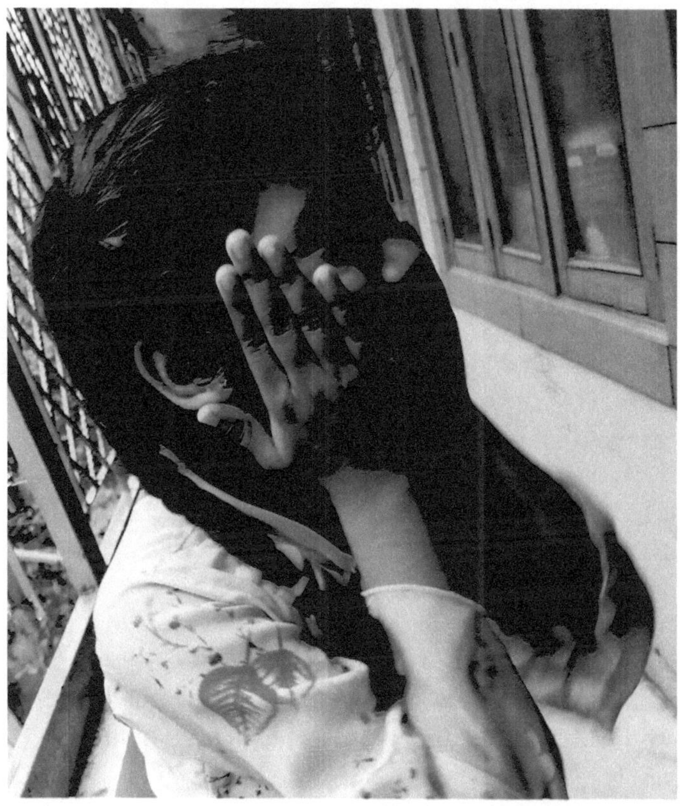

I was surprised; for a moment; -at what analysis of my life was about to take a new turn on my wounds.

I had decided to live; my battle fought with my pain and fear; had shown endurance, and patience; is this the result?

Truth and verdicts are judged not by talk but by logic.

The truth of what Karam's Uncle said could have been surrogated by going to his relative's house.

Everything was lost in two days of life, so now there was nothing left to lose. I also have to tell about those terrorists- those who I witnessed in the jungle that night. I was more relieved to have soldiers' parents. These days, I have learned a lot, understood, and acquainted with life; and still crave to know more.

When there is no fear of losing something, then, discover to obtain something... That is why I answered yes to Karam Uncle's question.

Karam's Uncle not only took up the task of bringing me a family but also gave his son clean clothes for me to wear.

The rider was ready to fly.

After travelling for a day, we reached Punjab from Kashmir. That house adopted me when I got welcomed into that house.

As his martyred son's name was Krishan Singh, they call, Krishan has come back into their life, saying that they distributed sweets in the whole village and from then onward my name became Leela Krishna.

Just like I have won my suspicion in those days, in the same way, I will win on my fear even today. In a few moments, the time will come to present my presentation. By the exclusion of fear and else, I have to say it to myself - yes, I am ready.

CHAPTER FIVE

On Stage

I move like a light emanating from everyone's eyes. I will not get this platform every day to keep thinking. I want to fix the moment today to be a complete success.

Even today, I am alone in the forest of this temple. I don't foresee any audience except sitting in that one seat from the soul of my past. I am my audience. She glanced at me with two eyes, Miss Bhandari Ma'am. I cannot spot the terror in those eyes now; I can see hope and encouragement in them. To date, our attitude was the reason for our fear. What I can see now is courage for her students and passion for their progress. In her eyes, dreams of our bright future are alive. By looking at her, I move ahead with confidence.

Today I have to listen to myself with my words.

The stairs of this stage are no bigger than those hurdles which I have crossed.

The darkness of this stadium is much brighter than those dark, dense forests.

Maa, Baba, Karam Uncle, Mom Dad

- Yes, I'm a fighter.

Good morning

Before I start, my first fall, I want to thank all my compatriots who have nominated me, to live the moment of the occasion.

And there it starts a new question on my wit when I get to know about my nomination. What to write about? Haha!! What must be the topic on which I could attract my goal audience? Thus, should I write about some science fiction to impress my khadus teachers? Ha! Or shall I go with political issues, which will enhance my presentation's weight and standard to impress my seniors? Well! These were formidable for me, so I figured to write some fun-loving dreams, those that would be more pleasing to hear for my peers. But that's not me.

I was calmly sitting in the corner of my room last night when my mother came near to me to help me out from my shallow, tense situation. She smiled and suggested that I write about the courageous soldiers of our country. The topic was superb, but imagination comes beautifully out when there are some experiences linked within it.

Though I was blank-minded, my mother helped me to write the entire presentation about soldiers of our country with a profoundly catchy title, 'Courageous life'. No doubt, the notes are outstanding. It's in my hand.

But I'm here not going to present it. Yes, you read it correctly. I don't want to impend what I'm not. All you know me as Leela Krishan Singh, the daughter of an army family. But there is a past hidden in my pretty name, the bean of Leela, only Leela. Because my late mother and father used to call me by this name with no other sign of thoughts; today in my words you will find out about another phase of my life, losses, survival, acceptance and learning. I am Leela Krishan, presenting Endurance: the survivor.

Why is this terror? This name
was not understood. That is wrong,
fearful, avoid this; parents had determined
solely here.
Why doesn't their core
frozen, while soaking the
colourful corridors in one colour?
Or their form does not have a heart,
creation has moulded them into a distinct
mould or they have no God at all.
Why is this, where is this,
and behind which face is this terror hidden?
In the contentions of freedom and claim;
Why wasn't this fright taught and prepared?
Why does the
History of theology
come out as soon as we
sprouts? Has society been so
frightened by the defiance of history?
Religion has
created by human
and framed for the goodness
of humanity. Do not terrorize it
with the game of myths.
They charge, what is
your religion? The blood
flowing out of the body, what
holds its morality? If you are of my
faith, then you get help, otherwise, go of
hither the door is restricted.
Do not eat anything
from someone unknown,
do not take anything from them;

When you were teaching this; should
not help any anonymous; why did you hide this?
The faces of these
terrorists are no different;
the same emotions spill on their
front as it is on me or your face. They
fearlessly walked around shamelessly, playing
the orgy of death.
Today, society is
afraid of helping someone.
Who knows, who enters the house
to kill them? To whom we are feeding
with love, the same may add poison to our
food and strength.
Every person is not
the same, do not panic,
neutral, be careful! Why to
discharged responsibility, by
saying this?
What is this
caution? Where do you
get this? Do tell us, we innocents,
about its address, which Dharam rope
pulls it well?
One day, to
compile the history
of us, why did they grow
up their head with a shroud?
WHY?
Why criminals
stand there, only, it's our,
It is our mistake here